TESSA KRAI

The Petsitters Club

3. Donkey Rescue

Inside Illustrations by John Eastwood

BARRON'S

First edition for the United States, Canada, and the Philippines published by Barron's Educational Series, Inc., 1998.

First published in Great Britain in 1997 by Scholastic Children's Books, Commonwealth House, 1-19 New Oxford Street, London WC1A 1NU, UK
A division of Scholastic Ltd

Barron's Educational Series, Inc.
250 Wireless Boulevard
Hauppauge, New York 11788
http://www.barronseduc.com

ISBN 0-7641-0572-8
Library of Congress Catalog Card No. 97-38857

Library of Congress Cataloging-in-Publication Data

Krailing, Tessa, 1935-
    The Petsitters Club. 3, Donkey rescue / Tessa Krailing.—1st ed.
        p.   cm.
    Summary: Jovan convinces the other members of the Petsitters Club that rescuing a sad looking donkey standing alone in the field is just as important as exercising a very energetic puppy.
    ISBN 0-7641-0572-8
    [1. Clubs—Fiction.   2. Donkeys—Fiction.   3. Dogs—Fiction.]
I. Title.
PZ7.K85855Do   1998
[Fic]—dc21   97-38857
                                                        CIP
                                                        AC

Printed in the United States of America
9 8 7 6 5 4 3 2 1

Chapter 1

"Not Our Business"

Jovan first saw the donkey from the window of the school bus.

He and Matthew were traveling back from a soccer game. Their team had lost 3 to 4, so everyone on the bus was in a bad mood, players and spectators alike. Matthew, who had been playing goalie, was especially depressed. He sat next to

Jovan, every now and then giving a muffled, agonized groan as he recalled the four goals he had let into the net.

Jovan did his best to comfort him. "It wasn't your fault," he said. "You did your best."

But Matthew only closed his eyes and groaned again. Eventually Jovan gave up trying to talk to him and stared out the window instead. When they reached Bakewell Avenue, on the outskirts of town, the bus slowed down, and that's when he saw the donkey.

4

It stood alone in a field with its head hung low. Jovan didn't usually like animals, especially ones that could kick and bite, but it worried him that the donkey looked so thin and miserable. Even from this distance, he could see its rib bones sticking out beneath the skin.

"Hey, Matthew," he said. "Do you think that donkey's all right?"

Matthew glanced briefly through the window. "What? Oh, yeah, I guess so."

"But it looks so sad."

"Donkeys always look sad," said Matthew. "They have naturally sad faces. It doesn't mean anything."

"Shouldn't we do something about it? The Petsitters Club, I mean. Shouldn't we investigate?"

Matthew shook his head. "Not our business. We're petsitters, not an animal rescue service. If you think the donkey's sick, you'd better tell your dad. He's a vet. He'll know what to do."

But Jovan knew exactly what his father would say. "*I'm too busy to go out looking for work, Jo. If the animal's sick, tell the owner to call my office.*"

By this time the bus had passed the field and the donkey was no longer in sight. But Jovan couldn't stop thinking about it. He kept remembering its sad face and how lonely it looked in the field by itself. Of course Matthew was right. It wasn't really a job for the Petsitters. But, he decided he would mention it to the others tomorrow, when they met at Sam's house.

"You're the last one," Sam told him as soon as she opened the front door. "Matthew and Katie have been here for ages."

"Sorry," he said. "But Dad had to go out on an emergency call so we were late having lunch. I came as soon as I could."

"Oh, never mind." She led the way into the kitchen. "It's just that I have some important news."

"And we're fed up with waiting to hear what it is!" Matthew's little sister Katie looked up from the floor, where she was playing with Monty, her pet centipede. "Sam wouldn't tell us until you came."

"Well, he's here now," said Matthew. "So go on, Sam."

Sam glanced a little nervously at the centipede. "I think I'd feel happier if Monty was back in his box. I can't concentrate while he's crawling around the kitchen."

"Oh, all right." Katie picked up the centipede and murmured to him, "It's only for a little while, Monty. You see, *some* people don't like creepy-crawlies, though I can't imagine why. Bye for now." She put him carefully inside the box and replaced the lid.

Sam breathed a sigh of relief "The news is that we've had another call about our advertisement. A man called to say he needs somebody to sit with his dog this afternoon while he and his wife go out. He says it goes crazy if they leave it alone in the house."

"What does he mean, 'it goes crazy?'" asked Matthew. "Does he mean just a bit crazy, or foaming-at-the-mouth sort of crazy?"

12

"I don't know," said Sam.

"Maybe he means that it barks a lot," suggested Katie.

"I don't know," Sam said again. "My dad took the call. We'd better go into the den and ask him."

They found Sam's father at his drawing board, working on a new cartoon. He didn't look too happy about the interruption.

"All I can tell you," he said with a sigh, "is that the poor man sounded as if he was at his wit's end. He said that every time he and his wife went out, the dog chewed everything in sight: the carpet, the curtains, chairs, papers, everything!"

"Maybe it's hungry," said Sam.

"Or just plain disobedient," said Matthew.

"Is it a very big dog?" Jovan asked nervously.

"He said it wasn't very big when he bought it," said Sam's father, "but it's growing bigger and bigger every day."

Jovan didn't like the sound of this at all. When Matthew and Sam had first thought up the idea of the Petsitters Club he had been reluctant to join, because, although his father was a vet, he found most animals a bit scary. He kept his distance as much as possible from the pets they were asked to petsit, and large, crazy dogs were exactly the type of pets he usually tried to avoid.

He quickly said, "There's another job I think we should do. Yesterday Matthew and I saw a donkey in a field. . . ."

"Oh, Jo!" groaned Matthew. "I already told you; it's not our business. If you think the donkey's neglected, you should report it to the ASPCA."

Jovan was silent. He wasn't sure the donkey was neglected. It had *seemed* sad and thin, but he'd only seen it for such a short time. How could he possibly be certain?

Sam turned to her father. "What was the man's name?" she asked.

He scratched his head. "Buster, I think. No, that was the dog. Hang on, I wrote it down somewhere...." He began fumbling through the papers on his desk.

"Ah, here it is. It's Foster. No wonder I got them confused. 'Mr. and Mrs. Foster, 23 Meadow Drive. Four o'clock.' There, that tells you everything you need to know."

Not quite everything, Jovan thought. Like how fierce was this crazy dog? And how big were its teeth? And did it only chew carpets and curtains and books— or did it also chew humans?

Chapter 2

Buster

Sam heard Buster long before she saw him. She heard him as soon as she and the other Petsitters opened the front gate of 23 Meadow Drive. She heard him even louder when she rang the doorbell.

"He must be a biggish kind of dog, I bet," said Matthew. "He has a biggish sort of bark."

Jovan groaned.

A plump little man opened the door. He had a pink face and a worried expression. "Hello, hello," he said. "You must be the Petsitters. Come inside, come inside."

No wonder he had to say everything twice, Sam thought. You couldn't hear him the first time because of the barking.

He led them into the living room, where an equally plump, pink-faced, worried-looking woman stood with her hat and coat on, ready to go out.

"We had to shut Buster in the kitchen," she explained. "I think he suspects we're leaving him."

"He hates being left alone, you see," said Mr. Foster. "One of us has to stay with him all the time, otherwise he does terrible damage. *Terrible* damage!"

"We only got him three weeks ago," said Mrs. Foster. "And since we discovered how much damage he did we haven't dared to go out together. But then we saw your advertisement on the supermarket bulletin board. '*Any pet looked after*,' it said, '*large or small. We are the experts.*' " She looked at them anxiously. "You're very young to be experts. Are you sure you'll be able to handle Buster?"

"Well, that depends," said Sam cautiously. But because she was being cautious, her voice was too soft to be heard above the barking. She raised it to shout, "THAT DEPENDS ON HOW FIERCE HE IS."

"Oh, he's not fierce," said Mr. Foster. "Not fierce at all. He's very, very friendly."

Mrs. Foster nodded. "Very friendly. That's the trouble. He loves people so much he can't bear to be left alone."

"I'll go and get him." Her husband disappeared.

The barking stopped.

Jovan cleared his throat. "I'm still worried about that donkey. We don't need four of us to look after one dog."

But nobody was listening. They were too busy looking at the black, bouncy, eager young dog who burst into the room, dragging Mr. Foster behind him.

"Oh!" exclaimed Katie, delighted. "He's only a puppy!"

"A very *big* puppy," Jovan muttered under his breath.

"He's a year old," panted Mr. Foster, struggling to keep hold of Buster's collar. "We thought he'd be a good guard dog, but he *welcomes* everyone who comes to the door."

At that moment, Buster managed to

break free. He launched himself at Mrs. Foster, knocking her hat off

"Oh dear, oh dear," she cried. "He's seen me wearing my outdoor clothes and guessed we're going out. Quick, grab his collar."

Matthew grabbed Buster's collar and held on to it for all he was worth. Katie held on to Matthew, as if to add her strength to his, and Jovan took cover behind a chair.

"I've got him," panted Matthew. "You'd better make a run for it."

"Okay, we will." Mr. Foster picked up his wife's hat. They both hurried into the hall.

"Wait!" Sam followed them to the front door. "How long will you be gone?"

"Not very long," said Mrs. Foster.

"We're going to visit my mother and she only lives around the corner."

"About two hours, I think," said her husband. "How much do you charge? We forgot to ask."

"There's no charge," said Sam. "We do petsitting as part of our school's community service project. You just have to sign a form to say we've done a good job, that's all."

"Well, that's wonderful!" said Mrs. Foster admiringly. "Don't you think that's wonderful, Howard?"

"Wonderful," agreed Mr. Foster. "So good to hear of children providing a service for older people."

"We don't really do it for the people," Sam said. "We do it for the animals. But of course the owners have to sign the form because the animals can't."

Sounds of a struggle came from the living room.

"Hurry, my dear!" Mr. Foster opened the front door. "Get right in the car."

The door closed behind them. Sam wondered why they were going by car if Mrs. Foster's mother only lived around the corner. Maybe they found walking difficult. They both were a bit over-weight.

She went back into the living room to find Matthew still grimly holding on to Buster's collar. "You can let him go now," she said. "They're gone."

Matthew let go of the collar.

As soon as he was free, Buster began to run around and around the room. He ran over the couch, under the table, behind the chair, between their legs, all the while grinning like mad, his pink tongue lolling out of his mouth.

"I think he wants to play," said Katie.

"The main thing is to stop him from chewing," said Matthew. "Here, Buster. Get away from that chair."

All of a sudden Buster jumped up and put his two large front paws on Matthew's shoulders, knocking him backwards.

"Oh, help!" called Matthew, struggling to sit up.

"Quick," said Sam. "There must be some dog toys around somewhere, a rubber bone or a ball. Jo, go into the kitchen and see what you can find."

Miserably, Jovan went into the kitchen. He looked inside Buster's basket, but couldn't see anything except a chewed-up cushion. He searched the cabinets and drawers but found no sign of a rubber bone or a ball—no dog toys anywhere.

"What a waste of time!" he muttered to himself. "Why are we looking after this stupid dog when we could be saving that poor little donkey? I don't think I want to be a Petsitter anymore."

And he marched back into the living room to tell the others his decision.

Suddenly, he was lying winded on the floor with Buster standing on his chest. "I don't . . ." he panted. "I don't want . . ."

"Well, Jo?" Sam demanded. "Did you find any toys?"

"No," he gasped. "And I don't want to be a . . ."

But he couldn't finish because Buster started licking his face.

"Oh, this is impossible!" exclaimed Sam. "Come on, everyone, think *hard*. Somehow we have to find a way to keep Buster occupied for the next TWO HOURS!"

Chapter 3

Walkies!

When Sam got home, she collapsed into a chair in the den.

"I'm exhausted!" she said. "Those were the longest two hours of my life."

Dad looked up from his drawing board. "Difficult dog?"

"Not difficult exactly. Just lively." She groaned. "He wanted to play all the time.

It wouldn't have been so bad if we'd found something for him to *play* with, but there weren't any dog toys around, not even a ball."

"No wonder he chews things," said Dad. "Sounds to me like he's bored."

"The worst moment was when Mr. and Mrs. Foster came home. They said that they had such a nice time with Mrs. Foster's mother that they'd like to go again next week."

"And they want you to sit with Buster?"

Sam nodded. "They seemed so grateful for what we'd done that we didn't want to say no. But *two hours!* You've no idea how long that is when you're looking after a dog like Buster."

Dad grinned. "I can guess. Why don't you take him out for a walk? That might calm him down a bit."

"Ye-es," said Sam doubtfully. Buster indoors was bad enough. Buster let loose on the big, wide world might prove to be a disaster.

On the other hand, it would help to pass the time. She decided to suggest it to Mr. and Mrs. Foster when they went next week.

"A *walk?*" Mr. Foster looked astonished. "You'd like to take Buster out for a *walk?*"

"If you wouldn't mind," said Sam. "We thought he might enjoy it."

Mr. Foster looked uncertainly at his wife. "What do you think, Rose?"

"I'm not sure," she said. "I don't know how he'd behave."

"Haven't you ever taken him out for a walk?" Matthew asked.

Mrs. Foster shook her head, "But we've taken him out in the car. Haven't we, Howard?"

"Once or twice," said Mr. Foster. "But he got so excited we thought it best to leave him at home."

Alarming noises came from the kitchen, bumps and scratches and short, sharp barks, as if Buster could hear what they were talking about.

Jovan cleared his throat. "My dad says that dogs need lots of exercise. Especially big dogs."

"His dad's a vet," Katie explained.

"But it doesn't matter if you don't like walking. We'll take Buster out for you."

Matthew nodded. "It's all part of our petsitting service. We're used to taking dogs out for walks. Do you have a leash?"

Mrs. Foster looked vague. "I seem to remember seeing one somewhere." She turned to her husband. "Howard, where did you put the leash that Buster's previous owners gave us?"

"In the hall closet, I think." He opened the door and peered inside. "Yes, here it is. It's one of those special expanding leashes. You have to press this button and, presto, it becomes very, very long."

"Oh, that's great!" said Sam. "That means we can keep it short while we're walking on the sidewalk and let it out long when we reach open ground."

Mr. Foster said doubtfully, "Are you sure you can manage him?"

"We're sure," said Sam.

When Mr. and Mrs. Foster had gone, Jovan said, "I'm still worried about that donkey. We don't need four of us to walk a dog."

"Oh, yes, we do," said Sam. "This isn't just *any* dog we're walking, remember. This is Buster." She opened the kitchen door. "Come on, Buster. Let's go for a walk!"

Joyfully Buster burst into the hall to greet them, and when they showed him the leash he nearly went crazy.

"I bet this is what he's wanted all along," said Matthew thoughtfully.

"Every time he saw Mrs. Foster putting on her hat and coat, he thought he was going out. That's why he got so excited."

Sam nodded. "But when he realized they were leaving him behind he was so upset that he started chewing everything up."

"I think it's cruel to keep a dog and not exercise it," said Katie.

"Hold still, Buster," said Matthew, clipping the leash onto the dog's collar.

"Okay, now where should we go for a walk?"

"Up to the park," said Sam. "He can have a good run there."

"Down to the river," said Katie. "So I can look for tadpoles."

"I know a better place," said Jovan.

They all turned to look at him.

"Where?"

"A field where he can really enjoy himself. It's up Bakewell Avenue, right on the edge of town."

"Okay," said Sam. "We'll walk up to Bakewell Avenue, then back along the path to the park. That way, everyone will be happy. With any luck, it'll use up the whole two hours."

Chapter 4

KEEP OUT.
PRIVATE PROPERTY

Jovan felt really pleased with himself.

The others had no idea why he had suggested walking up Bakewell Avenue, not even Matthew, who should have guessed because he'd been on the bus when they first saw the donkey. But they were all too busy worrying about

Buster to realize why Jovan wanted to come this particular way.

"He's very strong," panted Matthew, as Buster dragged him along. "I can hardly hold him."

"Let me take him," begged Katie.

"He'd knock you over," said Matthew. "What he wants is a good long run. How does this button work?"

"Here, give it to me," said Sam. "You have to press it like this, and then, oops!"

The leash shot out to its full length, about six feet, and Buster leaped forward, nearly knocking over an elderly lady. He dashed along the sidewalk and finally managed to wind himself and the leash three times around a lamppost.

"Oh, *Buster!*"

Sam and Katie tried to untangle him while Matthew apologized to the lady.

Jovan walked steadily on. He couldn't wait to get to that field again and find out if the donkey was all right.

"Better keep the leash short while we're walking along the road," Matthew said. "We can let it out when we get to some open ground."

"It seems a long way," Sam panted, as Buster pulled her along, straining at the leash. "How much further is this field, Jo?"

"Not very far," Jovan said.

At last they reached Bakewell Avenue.

"There it is!" Jovan began to hurry, and Buster, hearing the excitement in his voice, dragged Sam after him.

Jovan leaned on the fence, staring into the field. "It's empty," he said, when the others caught up with him.

"It's empty all right," said Sam. "But it's private land. We can't take Buster in there."

"It's a very muddy-looking field," said Katie. "Buster would get filthy."

"It's all my fault," muttered Jovan. "I should have come before."

The others stared at him. "What's your fault?" asked Sam.

"I knew he was sick, and now he's dead!"

"Who's dead?" asked Katie.

"The donkey." Miserably, Jovan gazed into the empty field.

Sam said, "So *that's* why you wanted to come this way."

"Of course!" Matthew exclaimed. "I should have realized this was the same field we saw from the bus."

"But you don't *know* that the donkey's dead, Jo," said Sam. "He could have been moved somewhere else."

"Why don't you go and ask?" suggested Katie.

Jovan shrugged. "Ask who?"

"The owners," said Sam. "I bet they live in that house over there. You could tell them you've seen the donkey in the field and wondered where it was."

"Yes, go on," urged Katie.

"We'll wait here, at the end of the driveway," said Matthew. "But don't be too long or Buster will get fed up with waiting."

"Good luck," said Sam.

Jovan set off up the rough path.

As he got closer to the house, he saw there were a lot of chickens running around the yard and some rather fierce-looking geese. On the gate was a large notice:

KEEP OUT
PRIVATE
PROPERTY.

He hesitated. What if the owners thought he was interfering? They might get angry. They might complain to his father. They might . . .

But then Jovan thought of the donkey. He was determined to find out what had happened to it. So determined that he opened the gate and marched straight up to the front door, scattering the chickens in his path. He rang the bell and waited.

A large, sloppy-looking woman answered, wiping her hands on a towel. "Yes?" she said. "What can I do for you?"

Jovan swallowed hard. "Er, I came about the donkey," he said. "The one that used to be in the field. I wondered, is he still alive?"

"Poor old Dillon? Yes, he's alive. He's over there, waiting to be sold." The woman nodded in the direction of a ramshackle barn. "Take a look if you like."

Jovan didn't particularly want to look. Donkeys were the kind of unpredictable animal he usually tried to avoid meeting at close quarters. They had large yellow teeth and back legs that kicked.

On the other hand, he knew he'd never forgive himself if he went away without making sure. A little nervously he approached the barn.

Chapter 5

Dillon

When he saw the donkey standing with its head hung low he forgot his fear and went straight up to it. Cautiously, he reached out a hand to touch its shaggy head. The donkey didn't move. Jovan ran a hand along its bony back, over the strange black marking in the shape of a cross that all donkeys have, and noticed there was a sore on its left shoulder.

"He's good with children." The woman spoke from behind him, making him jump. "That was his work, you see, giving rides to kids. But now he's too slow to keep up with the other donkeys."

Jovan stroked the tangled mane. No wonder the donkey looked so sad and lonely. He must be missing his friends.

"What's his name again?" he asked.

"Dillon. He's a good old boy, but my brother says we can't afford to keep him now that he's too old to work."

"Is that why he's going to be sold?"

She nodded. "The dealer's coming for him tomorrow morning."

Jovan's father had told him what happened when old animals were sold. Dillon might be lucky and find a good home; but because he was too old to work, he was far more likely to be sold for pet food. The idea was too horrible even to think about!

"Can I buy him?" he asked.

The woman looked surprised. "How much money do you have?"

"I, I have ten dollars in my savings account."

"Add another forty and he's yours."

"*Forty?*" Jovan stared at her. "But that makes fifty altogether. I can't afford fifty dollars."

"Ah, well." Regretfully the woman turned away.

"No, wait. I'll try to borrow the money."

She hesitated. Then she said, "Well, all right. But if you're not here by nine tomorrow . . . ."

Before she could finish, a terrible commotion started in the yard: a squawking and a honking and a flapping of wings.

"What's that?" She hurried outside.

Jovan stopped only long enough to whisper in Dillon's ear, "I'll save you. I promise," before following her.

When he saw the cause of the commotion he groaned, "Oh, no!" There was Buster, on the end of the leash, dragging Sam behind him. The big black dog raced around the yard, creating havoc amidst the geese and the chickens.

"Sorry, Jo," Sam called as she shot past. "I couldn't stop him."

The woman turned on him, looking furious. "Is that your dog? I warn you, if he upsets my hens . . ."

But Buster thought it was all a great game. He dashed here and there, barking loudly and making the geese very angry. They advanced on him, flapping their huge white wings. Buster suddenly got scared and tried to hide behind Sam. The trouble was that in running around her several times, pursued by the hissing geese, he managed to tie her up like a Christmas package.

"Help!" she called. "I can't move."

The woman shooed the geese away while Jo tried to unwind the leash. By this time, Matthew and Katie had arrived. They looked on with horror and disbelief.

At last Jovan disentangled Sam. "Quick," he said. "Shorten the leash."

But by now Buster was in such a panic that he tried to leap into her arms for protection, as if he were a puppy again.

Matthew came to help. "Buster, stand still!" he thundered.

Buster, taken by surprise, stood still. Sam shortened the leash and retreated with him to the other side of the gate.

Jovan turned to the woman. "I'm sorry," he said, "but he's not our dog. We were only taking him for a walk."

"I don't care whose dog it is," she snapped. "If you'd shut the gate properly, this wouldn't have happened."

Jovan blushed. "I'm very, very sorry," he said again. "And I'll try to get the money before nine tomorrow."

"Forget it," said the woman. "I'm selling Dillon to a dealer and no one else. Now please remove yourself and that lunatic dog from my premises—AT ONCE!"

She shut the gate firmly behind them.

"*And don't come back!*"

Chapter 6

Donkey Problem

Sam felt terrible. It was her fault that Buster had gotten into the yard and upset the chickens. Now Jovan had lost his chance of buying Dillon before he was sold off.

"We'll just have to go to the dealer ourselves," she said as they walked along the path, "and buy him. How much money do we need?"

"Fifty dollars," said Jovan hopelessly.

"*Fifty dollars?*" Sam stopped dead to stare at him.

"That's what *she* wanted. The dealer might ask more."

Katie said, "I have fifty cents you can have, Jo."

"I'm saving up for a computer," said Matthew, "but I can let you have two dollars."

"And I have ten dollars in my savings account, but that still only makes twelve dollars and fifty cents," said Jovan. "It's not enough."

Sam felt worse than ever. Jovan looked so desperate, yet she had nothing at all to offer him. Somehow she never managed to save a penny, and although it was only Sunday, she had already spent this week's allowance.

To cover her embarrassment, she said, "Buster's still got lots of energy. Let's go up to the park." And she set off at a fast pace, leaving the others to follow.

When they reached the park, she let out the leash as far as it would go and raced back and forth with Buster across the grass. Running was the best way she could think of to banish Jovan's donkey problem from her mind, because thinking about it made her unhappy. Soon she was out of breath and Matthew took over, then Katie, then Jo, and then it was Sam's turn again. After an hour, it was hard to tell who was most exhausted, the Petsitters or the dog.

"Can't we take him back now?" pleaded Katie. "I'm sure he's had enough exercise."

"Oh, all right," said Sam. They set off for Meadow Drive.

By the time Mr. and Mrs. Foster returned, everyone was sitting quietly in the living room. Even Buster was stretched out on the rug, and although he lifted his head and thumped his tail in greeting, he made no move to get up.

"What's the matter with him?" asked Mrs. Foster, alarmed. "Is he ill?"

"No, just tired," said Matthew. "We took him for a long walk and it's worn him out."

Mrs. Foster gazed wonderingly at Buster. "I've never seen him so quiet and calm."

"We think he probably only chews things up because he's bored," said Sam.

"He is a big dog. He needs plenty of exercise," said Matthew.

Katie said boldly, "We think you should take him out for a good long walk every day."

Mrs. Foster looked astonished. "Did you hear that, Howard? A long walk every day. That's just what the doctor said *you* should have. He said it would do wonders for your blood pressure."

"He said *you* should exercise more, too," said Mr. Foster. "He said it might solve your weight problem."

"Maybe we should leave the car at home sometimes and go for walks together?" said his wife.

"With Buster," Katie reminded them.

"We'll start tomorrow." They beamed at the Petsitters. "How smart you are!"

But then Mrs. Foster noticed their gloomy faces. "Is something wrong?" she asked.

Before Sam could stop herself she blurted out, "We need fifty dollars."

Mr. Foster looked taken aback. "But I

thought you didn't charge for petsitting. You said it was part of your community service project."

"It's not for the petsitting. We want to buy a donkey."

"A *donkey?*" Mr. Foster looked even more surprised. "Why do you want to buy a donkey?"

"To save it from being sold," said Jovan, "and being made into pet food."

"Oh, *don't!*" wailed Katie, clapping her hands over her ears.

"Maybe *you'd* like to buy it," Sam suggested. "Donkeys are very useful. You could keep him in your garden shed."

"Our garden shed's rather full at the moment," said Mrs. Foster. "Besides, we wouldn't know what to do with a donkey, would we, Howard?"

Her husband shook his head. "Fifty dollars is a lot of money. I'm afraid we can't help you."

Sam sighed deeply. "Oh, well. Would you please sign our community service form?"

"With pleasure." Mrs. Foster looked at Buster, who was still stretched out on the rug. "We're very grateful to you for making Buster so quiet and calm. I only wish we could help with your donkey problem."

It was a gloomy quartet of Petsitters who trudged down the path. "At least we've helped Buster," Matthew pointed out. "Even if we can't save Dillon."

"But we *must* save Dillon," said Jovan obstinately. "We just have to find a way."

"There isn't much time," Katie reminded him.

"Something will turn up, I know it will." He went off alone down the road.

As soon as Sam got home, she told her father what had happened. "I wish I wasn't so broke," she said. "I suppose it's no use asking you for forty dollars?"

"Afraid not," said Dad. "I'm even broker than you are."

She sighed. "There *must* be a way, I know there must!"

At that moment the telephone rang. Dad answered it, then held out the receiver to Sam. "It's Mrs. Foster," he said. "She says she's thought of a solution to your donkey problem."

Chapter 7

Sale Day

When Jovan remembered what day it was, he groaned and turned over in bed.

At breakfast his mother asked him why he didn't eat his cornflakes, but he only shook his head and pushed the plate away. She immediately put a hand on his forehead to see if he was feverish.

"I'm not sick," he assured her. "But it's

the day Dillon is going to be sold and I don't have enough money to save him."

His mother looked at him sorrowfully. "It's probably for the best," she said. "Buying a donkey is only the beginning. You'd have to pay for his keep as well."

Jovan knew this was true, but it didn't make it any easier.

The front doorbell rang. When he answered it, he found Matthew and Katie on the doorstep.

"Sam says we have to meet her in town," said Matthew.

"Her and Mrs. Foster," said Katie.

"Mrs. Foster?" Jovan was suddenly hopeful. "Has she changed her mind about buying Dillon?"

"I don't know," said Matthew. "Sam was a bit mysterious."

"She told us to get you, Jo," said Katie. "There might be other donkeys there and you're the only person who knows what Dillon looks like."

"Okay, I'm coming!"

In town, they found Sam standing beside a tall, bearded man and a woman in a scarlet track suit in a lot with animals in it. "Jo, this is Mr. Mackay," said Sam. "We've told him all about Dillon and he thinks he can save him."

The bearded man held out his hand. Puzzled, Jovan shook it.

"Isn't this exciting?" said the woman in the track suit. As soon as she spoke, Jovan realized it was Mrs. Foster. "After you left yesterday, I remembered Mr. Mackay and knew he'd be just the person to help."

"First I need to see the donkey," said Mr. Mackay. "Do you think you can find him, young man?"

Jovan looked around the lot. There were several horses and donkeys tied up beside vans. "I'm sure I'll recognize him," he said. "He was very thin, and he had a sore on his left shoulder."

"Okay, lead the way," said Mr. Mackay. "The rest of you had better stay here."

Mr. Mackay and Jovan walked slowly between the lines of trucks, looking at all the animals. Most of them were in fairly good condition, but at the very end of the line stood a sad little donkey with its head hung low.

"That's him," said Jovan in a low voice. "That's Dillon."

At the sound of his voice, Dillon raised his head. His dark eyes seemed full of pleading.

"Good," said Mr. Mackay. "Now go back to the others and leave this to me."

Jovan hated walking away, yet somehow he felt that he could trust Mr. Mackay.

When he reached the others, he turned around to see what was happening. He saw a man come out of the van and start talking to Mr. Mackay. They seemed to be having quite a long

discussion. Then Mr. Mackay took out his checkbook and rested it on the hood of the van.

"What's he doing?" asked Katie. "I can't see."

"I think he's writing a check," said Jovan.

"Yes, he is," said Sam. "He's buying Dillon!"

"Oh, wonderful!" said Mrs. Foster. "I knew he'd be able to help you."

"But who *is* Mr. Mackay?" asked Jovan. "And what's he going to do with Dillon?"

"Mr. Mackay runs the Donkey Sanctuary," said Mrs. Foster. "He'll make sure that Dillon's taken care of in his old age and has a happy retirement."

A slow smile spread over Jovan's face. He watched as Mr. Mackay came towards them with Dillon plodding quietly behind.

"You did the right thing to let us know about him," said Mr. Mackay. "He's in poor condition, I'm afraid, and it'll take us a while to nurse him back to health. But you can rest assured he's in safe hands now."

"Thanks, Mrs. Foster," said Sam. "That was a brilliant idea of yours."

Mrs. Foster beamed. "It was rather clever of me, wasn't it? Now I must go and find my husband and Buster. They're waiting for me by the road."

Sure enough, on the other side of the road stood Mr. Foster in a royal blue track suit with Buster straining at the leash. As soon as Mrs. Foster joined them, all three of them walked away together at a brisk pace, heading for the park.

"Looks like they're going for a walk," said Sam. "Buster will enjoy that."

Jovan stroked the donkey's head. "Can I come and see him?" he asked Mr. Mackay.

"As often as you want," said Mr. Mackay. "We could do with more sharp-eyed young people like you around. Any time you'd like to come and help out at the Sanctuary, you'll be very welcome."

"We'll all come!" chorused the Petsitters.

They watched Mr. Mackay lead Dillon into a van and drive away.

"I can just picture it, can't you?" said Sam with a happy sigh. "Dillon at the Donkey Sanctuary."

"With all the other donkeys," said Matthew.

"A big green field to graze in," said Katie.

"And a shed for shelter when it's cold," said Sam.

Jovan nodded. "He'll think he's in heaven!"

The End

This story is dedicated to Dillon and his friends at the Isle of Wight Donkey Sanctuary.

Join The Petsitters Club for *more* animal adventures!